OONA BRAMBLEGOOP's SIDEWAYS MAGIC

A Boy in the Fairy World

Look for all of the
Oona Bramblegoop's
Sideways Magic
books!

Newbie Fairy

A Boy in the Fairy World

OONA BRAMBLEGOOP'S SIDEWAYS MAGIC

A Boy in the Fairy World

written by
KATE KORSH

illustrated by
MARTA ALTÉS

putnam

G. P. Putnam's Sons

G. P. Putnam's Sons
An imprint of Penguin Random House LLC, New York

First published in the United States of America by G. P. Putnam's Sons,
an imprint of Penguin Random House LLC, 2024

Text copyright © 2024 by Kate Korsh
Illustrations copyright © 2024 by Marta Altés

Excerpt from *Fairies vs. Leprechauns* © 2025 by Kate Korsh

Visit us online at PenguinRandomHouse.com.

Library of Congress Cataloging-in-Publication Data
Names: Korsh, Kate, author. | Altés, Marta, illustrator.
Title: A boy in the Fairy World / by Kate Korsh; illustrated by Marta Altés.
Description: New York: G. P. Putnam's Sons, 2024.
Series: Oona Bramblegoop's sideways magic; book 2
Summary: "When a human boy follows Oona up into Blackberry Bog, it takes lots of
creativity and underwear magic to keep him safe"—Provided by publisher.
Identifiers: LCCN 2022051269 (print) | LCCN 2022051270 (ebook)
ISBN 9780593533666 (hardcover) | ISBN 9780593533673 (trade paperback)
ISBN 9780593533680 (epub)
Subjects: CYAC: Fairies—Fiction. | Magic—Fiction. | Boys—Fiction.
Classification: LCC PZ7.1.K6816 Bo 2024 (print) | LCC PZ7.1.K6816 (ebook)
DDC [Fic]—dc23
LC record available at https://lccn.loc.gov/2022051269
LC ebook record available at https://lccn.loc.gov/2022051270

Printed in the United States of America
ISBN 9780593533666 (hardcover)
ISBN 9780593533673 (paperback)
1st Printing
LSCC

Design by Nicole Rheingans
Text set in Cosmiqua Pro

*To the President and Vice President
of my fan club, aka Mom and Dad,
for always putting books in my hands*
—K.K.

For Grandma Sue
—M.A.

OONA BRAMBLEGOOP'S SIDEWAYS MAGIC

A Boy in the Fairy World

CHAPTER ONE

"Solid work tonight, little fairy," Oona said to herself. "You may not be important just yet, but you're getting there." She put her wand in its case, turned off her glow-worm lamp, and snuggled down into her nest, ready to snooze.

WOOOOOOP, WOOOOOOP, WOOOOOOP! CLANG, CLANG, CLANG, CLANG! The sound was deafening, but covering her ears only made it louder because the alarm was inside Oona's head. It was her extra fairy perception, or EFP for short, signaling a Level 13 emergency.

"Oof, not *now*," said Oona.

Oona Bramblegoop, otherwise known as the Underwear Fairy, had just returned from a full night of supplying magically protective underwear to clumsy children. Now all she wanted to do was pull a blanket of cloud fluff over her head and dream about

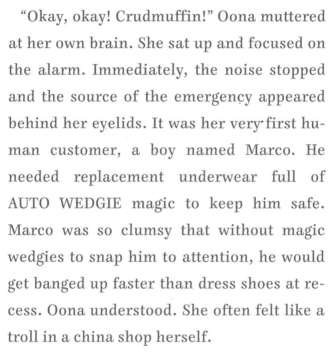

glitterberry cakes. Her EFP, however, had other ideas.

WOOOOOOP, WOOOOOOP—

"Okay, okay! Crudmuffin!" Oona muttered at her own brain. She sat up and focused on the alarm. Immediately, the noise stopped and the source of the emergency appeared behind her eyelids. It was her very first human customer, a boy named Marco. He needed replacement underwear full of AUTO WEDGIE magic to keep him safe. Marco was so clumsy that without magic wedgies to snap him to attention, he would get banged up faster than dress shoes at recess. Oona understood. She often felt like a troll in a china shop herself.

There was just one problem. The sun was about to peek over the horizon, and it was forbidden for fairies to leave Blackberry Bog in the daytime. The proper fairy thing to do would be to wait until nightfall, but Oona had never been very good at doing the proper fairy thing. Besides, if she waited until to-night, Marco would probably look like he'd been inside a giant pinball machine. If there was one thing Oona couldn't stand, it was the thought of her humans getting hurt.

Nope, she decided, she needed to go RIGHT NOW. If she hurried, she could get down there and restock his underwear drawer before he woke up.

Oona grabbed her wand and skimmed back down the staircase that wrapped around her tree, her wings helping so she stayed just above the steps.

At the bottom, she almost crashed into her little cousin Horace. Fortunately, he also wore

FUN FAIRY FACT: *Even though fairies can fly, they spend most of their time a few inches above the ground. The higher they go, the more tired their wings get. And since wings are also where magic is stored, most fairies like to keep their wings fully charged.*

magical underwear from Oona, so a wedgie scooted him backward and out of her way.

"Good morning, Oona! It's a great day to be a fairy, isn't it? Want to talk about slug stuff? Help me plan the slug spelling bee? The slug swim meet? Make slug snacks together?"

Horace had recently earned his first official job as Slug Fairy. Slug slime was the main ingredient in the coating that kept all of Blackberry Bog invisible to the human world. Since slugs were at their slimiest right after breakfast, Horace liked to get an early start on slime collection. He already had a slug on each shoulder and one on top of his head.

"Can't today, Cousin. Next time." Oona began flying toward the human world entrance.

"Where are you going? Isn't it almost bedtime for you?" Horace called after her.

"Emergency," Oona said over her shoulder.

"Emergency? What kind of emergency?"

The next thing she knew, Horace was right next to her, half running, half flying with his newly sprouted stubby wings.

"A bathroom emergency? You should probably head back to your nest. That's where the closest bath—"

"No, Horace! Not that kind of emergency." Ugh. Oona did not have time for this. But she knew Horace well enough to know that ignoring him wouldn't help. She stopped and explained the situation in as few words as she could.

"But . . ." Horace looked like she had told him that ice cream was extinct. "You can't go down there now. It's almost daytime! If the fairy council found out, you'd be suspended from magic for sure! And if a human saw you—"

"No one is going to see me. And as for the fairy council . . . well, are *you* going to tell the fairy council, Horace?" Oona raised her eyebrow and put her hands on her hips.

"Me?" Now Horace looked like Oona had said *Okay, ice cream's not really extinct, but the only flavor is mint chocolate booger*. "You know I would never!"

"Then they won't find out," Oona said simply. She started off again.

"I'm going with you," he said.

"No, you'll slow me down."

"I can help!"

"No."

"Fine. I won't go with you. I'll just go next to you at the exact same time."

Crudmuffin. There was no getting around the fact that stubbornness ran in their family. "Okay, you can come, but no more questions," she said. "Now, we've just got to make one quick stop."

Horace and his slugs followed as Oona darted into a willow grove and paused at the biggest, droopiest willow. They were in front of Lucy's house.

Lucy was not only Oona's best friend—she also happened to be the one and only Tooth Fairy. Oona pressed her finger to her lips. Horace nodded.

"Is Lucy coming with us, too?" Horace whispered.

"No, I just need to get her fairy dust. In case there's trouble."

"Wow. You think she's going to let you have her locket?"

"She doesn't have to let me. She's asleep."

"Wait. You're going to steal something from your best friend?" Horace wasn't whispering anymore.

"Shhhhhh! Horace, what did I say about questions?"

Horace stopped, cleared his throat, and said again, this time with a period, "You're going to steal something from your best friend."

"Not steal. Borrow. I'll have it back before she knows it's gone."

"Why not just ask her?"

Oona, pink with frustration, pulled Horace away from Lucy's nest. The truth was, she didn't want to ask because Lucy would probably say no. But Oona couldn't admit that.

"Because . . ." She smiled as she thought of a reason that showed how really good and generous she was being. "If she doesn't know, she can't get in trouble."

Horace pulled his eyebrows together, thinking hard about that one.

"Now, are you in or are you out?" Oona asked.

Horace looked like he had just decided to eat the booger ice cream. He bit his lip. "In."

"Great. You're on lookout duty. Stay here."
Oona flitted inside.

Oona crept past Lucy. Sure enough, she was
sleeping after her night of collecting teeth.
Oona loved her friend, but Lucy would never
understand what it felt like to be unsure if
you mattered. Lucy already had more tooth
customers than a leprechaun had tricks.
It was hard to figure out who loved her
more: the children of the world or the rest
of the fairies. She was the most popular
fairy of them all!

But Oona was a brand-new fairy with a
brand-new job, and finding customers had
turned out to be harder than she thought.
The biggest hitch was that most children
were just used to going to the Band-Aid
drawer a lot, and if they didn't know they
could use some help, then Oona's EFP didn't
light up. Oona was afraid the rest of the fairies wondered whether Oona's job was even
necessary. In fact, deep down, Oona wasn't

sure herself. But all she could do was take care of the children she *did* have on her rounds really, really well.

Yep. This was the only way. She scooped up the locket that lay on Lucy's nightstand and put it on.

Then she padded back outside and waved for Horace to follow her. Soon they were at the top of the magical twisty slide that connected Blackberry Bog with the human world.

Oona turned to Horace. His forehead was wrinkled with worry. Was this going to be too scary for him? She was his big cousin after all. She was supposed to protect him.

"Last chance to change your mind," she said to him gently. "After this, there's no going back. Are you ready?"

"Ready to break the number one fairy rule and go into a strange land filled with giant creatures after sort of stealing the prized possession of the most important fairy ever?"

"Pretty much, yes."

Horace squeezed his eyes shut and took a deep breath. Then he opened his eyes. "Ready," he said. "Besides, what could go wrong?"

࿊ ✦ ࿊

CHAPTER TWO

Horace had never been outside Blackberry
Bog before, so it was hard to get him to
hurry. He kept stopping to exclaim about
the hardness of the sidewalks, the tallness
of the buildings, and the stinkiness of the
trash cans (worse than troll breath!). Oona
hadn't been coming to the human world
for very long, but already all these things
seemed normal to her. So Horace kept
saying, "Wow!" while the slugs

did somersaults on his shoulders, and Oona would say, "Yes, wow." Then she'd grab his hand and give him a good tug.

When they got to Marco's yard, the birds were just starting their songs. Oona lifted her wand to buy them a little more time:

"We hope no feathers
will be ruffled.

These sweet, sweet songs
must now be muffled.

Not forever,
just a tweak,

Give each bird
a quiet beak."

She flicked her wand, and every bird in
the yard suddenly found themselves with
a spiral rainbow lollipop in their mouth.
Oona's magic always came out a little sideways like that. But at least they were quiet.
And loving their lollipops.

"Now, no flying, birdies! You need to sit
still when you have a lollipop. Safety first!"
Horace whispered helpfully. The birds nodded and stayed perched on their branches.

Oona and Horace landed on Marco's windowsill and peered into the hushed room. He was still in bed, his blanket pulled up over his head. Perfect.

"Okay, Horace, your post is this windowsill. Keep an eye on the bed. Any movement, alert me. Understand?"

"Aye, aye, Captain!" Horace said, saluting. "I'll keep an *eye, eye* on him. Get it?"

"I get it." Oona sighed. She slipped into the room and down to the dresser.

As soon as she opened the bottom drawer, she saw the problem. The magic underwear had more holes than a mini golf course! She held them up for Horace to see, but he was too busy. One of the birds had gotten her lollipop stuck to her wing, and Horace was trying to unstick it. Oona shook her head. Horace was a loyal fairy, but a lousy lookout. He just couldn't resist helping little creatures.

Oona turned back to her work. She raised her wand.

"Singers need songs
and dancers need dance.

We all need undies
up under our pants.

Before the clock's
alarm bell tolls,

Replace this pair
so full of holes!"

Instantly, new undies appeared on the end of Oona's wand, hanging from one point of the star.

FUN FAIRY FACT: *Fairy wands come in five models: Classic Sparkle Star, Moondoggle, Horseshoe and Heart, Lightning Up, and Basic Bagel. Classic Sparkle Star is the most popular, but recently Basic Bagel has been selling like hotcakes, or more accurately, like bagels.*

She plucked them off and placed them neatly in the drawer. But as she picked up the old undies again to get rid of them, she noticed something about the holes. They were just a little too perfect, almost as if they had been snipped with a pair of scissors. Why would anyone do that?

Oona started to get a twisty feeling in her tummy. "Oh no, Horace," she said. "Something's not right. I think this might be a—"

Suddenly, a cage made of Popsicle sticks and dental floss fell from a hook in the ceiling, right on top of Oona.

"Trap."

CHAPTER THREE

"Score!"

Marco was sitting up in bed, holding the other end of the string attached to the cage.

Oh no. Marco had trapped her! But why? What would he do next?

She needed to magic herself out of there immediately, but when she started to think of a spell, she noticed her hands were empty. Her wand had been knocked away by the falling cage and now lay out of reach on the other side of the bars. Double oh no.

Maybe Horace could help her! Oona looked up to the windowsill where Horace had been, but it was empty. Infinity oh nos!

"I've got you!" Marco said. He scrambled

out of bed and lay on the floor so his big head was even with the cage. "Hello, fairy lady. I'm Marco. It's a pleasure to finally officially meet you."

This friendly introduction after the business with the cage made Oona go from alarmed to grouchy. She crossed her arms over her chest. What kind of *thank you for the magic underwear* was this?

"We are not meeting," she said as calmly as she could. "Because I don't even exist. You just have a very good imagination."

Marco giggled and shook his head. "Oh no you don't. You can't fool me. I knew you were real the first time I saw you months ago, when you and your friend brought me underwear. When I wore it, I stopped getting hurt all the time. That's because of you!"

In spite of the trouble she was in, Oona couldn't help feeling a little charge of pleasure. She had never gotten appreciation from a human before.

But then Marco's smile faded. "No one believes me. They think I'm lying about you just to get attention. Well, now I have proof! I should get a picture." He stood up, went to his closet, and started rummaging around for his camera.

This was her chance. Oona popped open the locket and dumped its contents into her hand. But instead of a sparkling mound of fairy dust, she got a big, fat fistful of nothing. The locket was totally and infuriatingly empty.

FUN FAIRY FACT: *The source of fairy dust is a mystery. It's harvested by Grands, the oldest and wisest fairies, who keep the process a secret. The Newbies like to say that fairy dust actually collects in the corners of the Grands' eyes when they fall asleep during boring fairy council announcements, and that's why the dust makes humans sleepy and forgetful. The Grands do not appreciate this rumor.*

Flattening herself against the bars, Oona strained her arm through the cage toward her wand. No luck. She tried reaching with her leg. Then she tried reaching with her other leg. Unfortunately, both of her legs were the same size.

"Aha!" Marco pulled his camera from under a pile of stuffed animals and pointed it at Oona. "Smile!"

Oona did not smile. Instead, she tried as hard as she could to look less real, like a fairy toy or even a drawing of a fairy, but

it was very hard to look two-dimensional, especially considering her dimples and nice round tummy.

"Shoot, why isn't it working? The batteries must be dead. Don't move, fairy. I'll be right back." Marco headed out of the room in search of more batteries.

Oona turned back to her wand and yelped with relief. The three slugs that had come down the slide with Horace were there! They had hoisted the wand on top of where shoulders would be if slugs had shoulders and were sliming their way toward her.

"You guys are the best!" The wand felt cool and smooth in her hand. She lifted it toward the sky.

"Cats are like lions but not quite as fierce. And some types of monkeys have colorful rears.

Slugs are a *whole lot*
more *slippery* than me,
But I have to slip out of here
and be *free!*"

"Whoa, whoa, whoa!" Oona's feet suddenly slid out from under her, and she landed on her bottom. Immediately, her butt felt very cold. She looked down to see that the floor had turned to ice. It seemed this is what sideways magic did with the word *slip*. Oona sighed. What about the *free* part?

We're not laughing at you;
we're laughing with you.

Oona was going to have to do this the old-fashioned way. She slid over to the bars and set to work on the dental floss, trying to untie the knots that held the Popsicle sticks together. But the waxy coating seemed to seal each knot, and Marco would be back any second with fresh batteries! The slugs scooted over and tried to help her, but without fingers, they just made the knots slimy.

Oona bit her lip and blinked away the tears that were gathering. Why hadn't she thought this through? She should have followed the rules. She could have been safe in her nest right now. And how could Horace have just left her at a time like this? They were supposed to be family. Did he run away because he hadn't been a good lookout? Or was he just being a scaredy-fairy?

The tears were coming too fast now, and she couldn't see what she was doing. She picked up her wand and hit the bars with it.

Sparks flew out and sizzled as they sank into the ice by her feet. But the cage stayed put.

"Don't break your beautiful wand, fairy friend! We need it for the picture."

Marco was back. And he was determined to get his proof.

CHAPTER FOUR

"Let's talk about this, Marco," Oona
tried, wiping her nose. "Just lift this cage off
me, and then we can figure out together how
to get you what you need."

"Okay, sounds good," said Marco. Oona
exhaled. Then he said, "Let me get a quick
shot first, though. Ready? One, two—"

Just then, the bird with the sticky wing
soared through the window with Horace
on her back, riding her like a pony. The

bird flapped around Marco's head until he dropped the camera and covered his face with his hands.

At the same time, Lucy appeared in front of the trap. Oona had never been so happy to see someone in her whole life. The minute Lucy flicked her wand, all the dental floss strands untied themselves and stacked together in a neat pile. The Popsicle sticks collapsed around Oona.

"Why couldn't I do that?" Oona said. "That floss wouldn't budge for me."

Lucy shrugged. "Floss is teeth stuff. Teeth are my thing. If I ever get caught in a trap made of underwear, I'll be sure to call you." She tucked the floss in her pocket. "And speaking of underwear, did you wet your pants?"

"What? No!"

"Then why are you standing in a puddle?"

Lucy was right. Oona's magical ice had melted, and now her fairy slippers were soaked. "It's a long story," Oona said.

"Wet clothes always are," said Lucy.

Marco had thrown a blanket over his head

to protect himself from the bird, and now he was staggering blindly toward them.

"Let's go!" Lucy said. Oona scooped up the slugs and followed her out the window, the bird close behind them.

When they had all landed on the lawn, Horace gave the bird a thank-you pat and jumped into the grass.

"I thought maybe you'd left me," Oona said to Horace.

"Never! I went to get backup," said Horace, smiling at Lucy.

"Thank you," Oona whispered, leaning into a group hug.

"He did the right thing," said Lucy. "Escapes like that take a team." Suddenly, Lucy noticed her locket around Oona's neck. "And speaking of doing the right thing—"

Oona touched her neck. "Yeah, um, crazy story about that. You'll never believe how I got it. I, uh, I just found it outside your house. You must have dropped it. It seemed only right for me to keep it safe for you." Oona could feel Horace staring at her, his mouth open. "I mean," Oona faltered, "I mean . . ."

Lucy frowned. "You know what? You can explain it all when we're safe. Now, let's get back home and figure out what we're going to do about Marco."

The three fairies wasted no more time and were soon sliding upward.

They were halfway there when the twisty slide began to shake.

"Is this normal?" Horace asked.

"No!" Lucy and Oona said at the same time.

Lucy craned her neck over the side. "Holy cavities! Looks like we've got company."

Just then, Marco's voice came floating up. "Fairy friends! Wait for me!"

"Go faster!" squeaked Horace.

Lucy shook her head. "We can't beat him. We've got to *stop* him."

Oona raised her wand. "Let me handle this."

"Fine, just keep it simple."

"You got it," said Oona.

"He's too big,
and we're too small.

We don't want him
here at all.

As long as something
breaks his fall,

Send him home
from this close call."

Suddenly, the part of the slide that Marco was on broke off from the rest. It rocketed into the air like it had been shot from a cannon. Then, just before it hit the ground, it transformed into a magic carpet beneath him and began coasting.

Phew. "Just like I planned," said Oona.

"Are you sure?" asked Horace, pointing. Marco came cruising past them on the carpet. He looked like he was having a blast. Unfortunately, he was also shrinking. Uh-oh.

"Why did you have to say *small*?" Lucy said.

Oona cringed. "Because *super awesome* is hard to rhyme."

When Marco was about the size of a pineapple, the shrinking stopped.

But then things got worse. Much worse.

The magic carpet shot straight into Blackberry Bog.

FUN FAIRY FACT: *The part of the magical twisty slide that sits in the human world is almost always ignored by children because of its "Goldilocks" feature. The slide looks too scary for little kids to climb and too boring for big kids to climb, so children avoid it and miss the entrance to the fairy world altogether.*

CHAPTER FIVE

"I meant *his* home, not *our* home!" Oona grumbled at her wand as the three fairies zipped up the slide. "Marco, wait!"

The magic carpet was waiting at the top, but Marco was long gone. Even though he was now a fraction of his usual size, he was still much bigger than the fairies. He could cover a lot of ground fast.

"The fairy council is not going to like this," said Horace.

"Tell me something I don't know. We've got to get him back down the slide," said Oona.

"That's going to be tough since it's missing a piece now," said Lucy.

Oona cringed again. That was also her fault.

"But what will happen when Marco's parents realize he's missing?" asked Horace.

Oh no. Having a child make contact with fairies was bad enough, but adults were way more dangerous. They were too practical, too logical, and too boring. An adult confronted with real magic could blow half of fairydom to smithereens just with the force of their disbelief.

"Let's not worry about that yet," said Lucy. "It's Snorgleday after all."

Snorgleday came between Sunday and Monday in Blackberry Bog. Since Snorgleday didn't even exist in the human world, none of this time was passing down there.

They just had to solve the whole mess before the day was over.

Marco seemed so excited about exploring that it would have been hard to catch up with him, except he kept tripping and falling down. The fairies passed a broken bridge, a banged-up barn, and a worse-for-wear wishing well, all damaged by an excited, clumsy boy. They finally found him sitting, dazed, with the top section of a windmill perched on his head like a cap, propeller spinning.

"Are you okay?" Horace asked, climbing onto Marco's knee to examine the bump on his forehead.

"I mean, my head hurts a little, but how cool is this place? The sky is purple!"

"Of course it is," said Oona.

"Everything has glitter on it!" said Marco.

"What else would it have?" said Lucy.

"And," said Marco. "Do I smell cotton candy?"

"Well, sure," said Horace. "The windmill—or what used to be the windmill—powers our cotton candy factory. Cotton candy is one of the four fairy food groups."

While Horace explained how cotton candy was made, Lucy turned to Oona. "Look, we've got to fix the slide, unshrink Marco, and get him back down to the human world before he ends fairy life as we know it or the fairy council finds out or both," she said, ticking off a to-do list on her fingers.

"I know," said Oona, biting her lip. "But how?"

"First things first, Oona. You've got to make him new underwear so he doesn't break every building in the bog."

FUN FAIRY FACT: *The four fairy food groups are cotton candy, chocolate chip cookies, marshmallows, and ice cream. A healthy fairy breakfast is scrambled marshmallows with a glass of cookie juice. Of course, fairies also eat brussels sprouts every new moon to grow strong wings. And glitterberries are the traditional fairy dessert.*

Oona exhaled with relief. Now, that was something she could do. Oona whispered quickly—

"We just need one more new pair
Of Marco's safety underwear.
Because more bumps and bruises
Is never what he chooses."

That was a good spell, simple and clean, thought Oona. The underwear appeared without a hitch. She brought it over to Marco.

"That's fascinating. But can I try some?" Marco was saying to Horace.

"Of course—" Horace started.

"After you put on these new undies," Oona said. "Undies first, then cotton candy."

"But I can't put them on right now," said Marco, frowning.

"Why not?" asked Oona. Why were even easy things hard today?

"I'm too big for everything around here. Where would I change?" Marco crossed his arms. "I need privacy."

Oona paused. Privacy *was* important.

Then Horace said, "Just put them on over your shorts!" as if that were the most natural thing in the world. The other three laughed.

Horace shrugged. "I'm serious."

"But I'll look silly," said Marco.

"We won't laugh. We promise," said Lucy. "Right, fairies?"

"Right," the other two said.

Marco still looked doubtful, but he pulled on the underwear.

He looked so silly that Oona had to press her fairy fingernails into her

palms to keep from breaking her promise. But then Marco started grinning and snapping the waistband of the undies, and soon he was laughing so hard he had to sit down.

"Don't get a muddy butt on your new undies," said Horace, and they all collapsed into a fit of giggles.

Marco was just catching his breath when something caught his eye back the way they had come. "Oh, look!" he said.

Since he was so much taller, the rest of the group could not see what he saw.

"Look at what?" asked Horace.

"More fairies!" said Marco, clapping his hands with excitement.

Lucy and Oona stared at each other. "More fairies?" Oona squeaked.

Lucy sped down the path and peeked around the bend. When she came back, her face was serious.

"It's Molly. And she's coming this way."

Oona shuddered. Molly was the head of the fairy council. If she found out about Marco, Oona would get so punished she wouldn't be able to even look at a wand, much less use it. But what could they do?

CHAPTER SIX

"I want to meet Molly!" said Marco.

"NO!" shouted all three fairies at the same time.

Oona added, "She's very strict. You wouldn't like her. And she definitely wouldn't like you."

For the first time, Marco looked a little worried.

"You've got to hide or we are all going to be in more trouble than a baby tooth with a bag of taffy," said Lucy.

"Where?" Marco looked around for a hiding place, but everything was so small.

Oona started to raise her wand, then lowered it again. They didn't have time for sideways magic. Lucy's magic was much more reliable. "Quick, Lucy, your wand!" she said.

Lucy bit her lip. "He's already got your shrinking spell and your underwear protection. I don't know what my magic would do mixed up with all that."

Horace was breathing in big gulps. "Do something! She's almost here!"

Suddenly, Lucy's eyes lit up. "Do you like swimming, Marco?"

"Sure. Why?"

"Trust me."

She hustled him into the bog pond, which only came up to his knees. "Now, lie down so all of you is underwater." She picked up a hollow reed. "Hold this in your mouth and stick the end into the air to breathe."

"I feel like a spy," Marco said.

"Exactly!" said Lucy. "You're a mystery spy."

"Except my disguise is mud!" said Marco.

Just then, Molly's voice floated across the pond to them. "This is worse than I thought. Look at the poor barn!"

"Now, now, now!" Oona said. Startled, Marco flopped down into the water and muck. The surface had just stopped splashing and rippling when Molly flitted up next to Lucy, Oona, and Horace. Horace pressed his lips together like the secret was sitting on his tongue, fighting to get out.

"Hello, Lucy. Hello, minor fairies," Molly said as two other fairy council members arrived on either side of her.

"Hello, Molly," Lucy said, like the name tasted yucky.

"We are investigating vandalism. Have you seen anything suspicious come this way?" asked Molly. "Tornado? Runaway bulldozer?"

"Nope. Nothing out of the ordinary. Nothing at all. Only boring things have come this way. Like you. Not that you're boring. Just that you wouldn't be something that could get us in trouble. Why would we get in trouble?" said Oona.

"Stop talking now," Lucy whispered.

"Gladly," said Oona, exhausted.

Molly pulled out a large magnifying glass and peered at Oona through it. To Oona, Molly's eye now looked as big as a Frisbee. Oona shrunk backward.

One of Molly's companions, a mostly magenta fairy with long, thin fingers and long,

thin hair, wandered toward the edge of the pond. Then she said, "Aha!" and pointed at a very large footprint in the mud.

Molly turned her Frisbee eye from Oona's face to the footprint. Then she put the magnifying glass away, took out a notebook, and scribbled something.

"Giants haven't been seen in Blackberry Bog for many moons," she said. "How could this be?" With a snap, she magicked up a little puff of cloud, stepped onto it, and began floating over the water, scanning the surface.

Horace started jumping around like he had to go to the bathroom. His lips were pressed so tightly they turned a little purple.

"What are you doing, Molly? There's nothing in the pond but slugs," said Lucy. Molly ignored her, focusing on a group of bubbles rising from the water—*BLOOP, BLOOP, BLOOP!* She brought out her magnifying glass again.

Now she was almost directly on top of Marco! The reed he was breathing through was poking out just a few feet in front of the cloud puff. Oona couldn't stand it anymore.

"Yes, that's right! There was a giant! I saw it!" Oona cried. "It had three eyes! And hair coming out of its ears! And it was wearing . . . a sweater-vest!"

At that horrible notion, everyone gasped, including Lucy and Horace.

Molly zoomed her cloud over to Oona and jumped down.

"If a giant is in the area, we must capture it immediately. Alert the rest of the fairy council," she said to the mostly magenta fairy. "Put guards on every road. Set alert level to High. No one will move a muscle without us knowing exactly what they're up to."

Molly hustled away with her helpers, still barking orders. Oona, Horace, and Lucy watched them go.

"Looks like Operation Get the Boy Out of Blackberry Bog just got a whole lot harder," said Lucy.

FUN FAIRY FACT: *Blackberry Bog is home to many magical creatures besides fairies. Elves, trolls, leprechauns, brownies, and ogres can also be found there. Ogres are actually very sweet, and they love to give hugs and high fives. They only got a bad reputation because they are allergic to humans, so whenever they find themselves in the human world, they get terribly itchy and grumpy.*

Giants, however, do not belong in Blackberry Bog, and they do NOT give high fives.

‹ ✦ ›

CHAPTER SEVEN

"If only you had kept your locket stocked with fairy dust, none of this would have happened!" said Oona, throwing her hands up.

"Are you saying this is *my* fault?" said Lucy. "What about your rule breaking? And mess making? And *lying*?"

This was too much for Oona. She flopped cross-legged on the ground and hid her face. Lucy was right about all of it.

"I'm so sorry!" Oona snuffled into her hands. "No matter how much I try to help,

I just make everything worse." Horace came up behind her and began petting her hair. Oona let out a sob.

Then Lucy knelt down next to her. "Hold on, hey, it's not as bad as all that. We know you don't mean to make things go so sideways."

Oona leaned her head onto her friend's arm. "If it weren't for me, you'd still be cuddled in your bed, snoozing. And now we're in a hopeless situation!"

"Maybe not so hopeless," said Lucy, standing and pushing up her sleeves. "I like a challenge. Especially when it includes out-fairying Little Miss Molly. But," she added, "I'm going to need my locket."

Oona quickly pulled it over her head and handed it to Lucy, embarrassed. "I really am sorry—" she started.

Lucy waved her hand. "I know. Next time just ask me, okay?"

Oona nodded.

Horace tapped her on the shoulder. "Should we maybe get Marco out?"

"Oh, crudmuffin! Marco!" Lucy and Oona said together. Then Oona thumped her wand on the ground, signaling his underwear to give him a wedgie that pulled him out of the water. Marco sat up, an algae mustache across his face and water dripping from his hair.

"Was I a good spy?" he asked.

"You were great!" said Oona. "The only thing that almost gave you away were those bubbles."

Marco looked bashful. "I had to toot a little. A lot," Marco said.

"It happens," said Horace. The other two fairies nodded.

"Can I get that cotton candy now?" asked Marco.

"Yes," Lucy said. "But your spy mission isn't over. You have to stay incognito."

"Where's Cognito?" he asked as he squeezed water out of his shirt.

"No, *incognito* means disguised, out of sight. And not in the pond, either. Molly is already suspicious of it after she saw your toot bubbles. These two will help you with some special spy tricks." Lucy winked at Oona and Horace. "Now, I'm going to go see if I can fix the twisty slide." And off she flew.

Oona looked at Marco. It was time to make the biggest creature in Blackberry Bog disappear.

FUN FAIRY FACT: *Fairy toots smell like cinnamon. Unless, of course, the fairies actually eat cinnamon. Cinnamon multiplied by cinnamon equals asparagus toots.*

CHAPTER EIGHT

At first, Oona thought they could hide Marco under the drooping branches in the willow grove, behind the curtains at the Grand Fairy Theater, or under the Tricky Troll Bridge. But every time they started toward one of her hiding places, they had to turn back. There were fairies on the roads, fairies on the paths, fairies in every doorway. And they were all on the lookout for giants, thanks to her lie.

She would have to use magic. Oona had never done an invisibility spell before; that magic was usually left to the Grands. But how hard could it be?

While Horace went to find Marco some cotton candy, Oona began brainstorming her spell. Finally, she raised her wand and said:

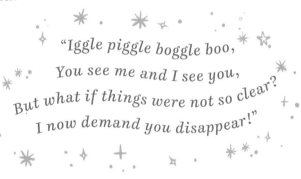

"Iggle piggle boggle boo,
You see me and I see you,
But what if things were not so clear?
I now demand you disappear!"

FUN FAIRY FACT: *The Grands do the most important job in Blackberry Bog: They mix their magic with slug slime to make the entire underside of the fairy world invisible, which is why humans can't see it in the sky. The spell is powerful and exhausting, so the Grands recharge with a lot of karaoke and Shirley Temples.*

She looked up. No Marco! Instead, there were dozens of pigs standing on one another's backs to make a pig pyramid. Had she turned Marco into a pig?

"Marco?" she asked the fattest pig, whose eyes twinkled a lot like Marco's. But then Marco stepped out from behind the pig tower. Phew. The pigs tried to shuffle in front of him again to block him from view.

"Yikes. The only thing more noticeable than a human is a pyramid of pigs," said Oona.

"I have an idea," said Horace, returning with a huge batch of cotton candy. He balled up several handfuls and threw them as hard as he could. Oinking and snorting, the pigs shuffled after it.

Marco helped himself to a big handful, too. "Mmmm, ten out of ten. And pig-approved."

"Let's try again, Oona," said Horace. "But this time, do what you do best!"

"What do you mean?"

"Remember when I turned a barrel of slug slime I was collecting into a fairy hot tub?"

Oona wrinkled her nose. She had been the Slug Fairy before Horace, but she had never loved slug slime the way he did. "How could I forget?"

"And remember what happened to my butt when I got in that hot tub while wearing a pair of your magic undies?"

Oona clapped her hands together. "It disappeared!"

She lifted her wand with a flourish.

"One potato, two potato,
three potato, four,

I often want one pair of these,
but now we want some more.

I'll make him disappear
with the help of my smart cousin,

So keep the undies coming
'cause we need at least two dozen!"

*GLIMMER, SPARK! GLIMMER,
SPARK!* One after another, pairs
of underwear began jumping off
the end of Oona's wand until there
was a pile at her feet.

"What are those for?"
asked Marco.

"You're going to wear
them," said Oona.

"All of them?" asked Marco.

Oona and Horace grinned
at each other. "All of them,"
they said.

CHAPTER NINE

They got to work, pulling and pushing Marco's limbs through a series of underwear holes.

When they were finished, Marco had three pairs of underwear going up each arm, four going up each leg, one wrapped around each shoe, a pair tucked into his shirt collar like a napkin, another on his back, and, of course, the pair he had already been wearing on the outside of his shorts.

"Now, the final touch," said Oona, and she flew up by Marco's face and pulled a pair of undies over his head so that an eye peered through each leg hole.

Then she and Horace stepped back to admire their work. Marco looked, well, completely ridiculous.

"It's perfect," Oona said, satisfied.

"But you can see me," said Marco. "Aren't I supposed to be invisible?"

"Just wait," said Horace. He whistled, but no sound came out—at least none the three of them could hear. It was a slug call, a whistle at a pitch only heard by slugs.

Sure enough, within seconds, a steady stream of slugs came scooching up out of the bog.

"Friends," said Horace to the slugs, "you know what to do. Slime him!"

The slugs turned toward Marco and began sliding up his legs. Marco started to giggle.

"Try to hold still," said Oona.

"I can't. It tickles!" Marco did a little dance. "Boy, this had better work," he managed to get out between bursts of laughter.

"It already is," said Oona, pointing. "Look!"

Marco looked down at his feet, or rather, where his feet used to be. Now he seemed to be floating on his kneecaps, and those were

fading away, too. After a minute, all that was left of Marco were his eyes, blinking wide with amazement.

"Pull your underwear mask down a little," said Oona.

He disappeared altogether.

Horace and Oona high-fived. The slugs gathered around Horace. He thanked each one with a little pat on their antennae, then sent them back into the bog.

"What's next?" asked Horace.

"We wait for Lucy," said Oona.

"Since I'm invisible, could we maybe explore some more?" asked Marco.

Oona considered this. "You're literally covered in protection, so you shouldn't break anything else. And no one can see you." She shrugged. "I don't see why not."

"Welcome to Blackberry Bog!" said Horace. "Allow us to be your tour guides."

CHAPTER TEN

For most of the afternoon, Oona and Horace showed their new friend all the wonders of Blackberry Bog. They went to Fairy Beach, where the sand is made of sprinkles. When Marco held a shell to his ear, he could hear the mermaids sing.

Then they picked blackberries out of the bramble and fed them to the unicorns in Glitter Gulch. They even went to Rainbow Road, where the leprechauns live, and watched the blacksmith make iron pots for all their gold.

FUN FAIRY FACT: *A popular activity at Fairy Beach is Ask the Fortune Teller, where fairies throw a yes-or-no question in a bottle into the waves. At the next high tide, the bottle will float back with one of six possible responses: "One billion percent," "As surely as fairies fly on Frimpday," "How the heck should I know," "Not on your life," "How dare you," and "Ask again after you've eaten some brussels sprouts."*

Finally, they had come full circle. They paused by the broken windmill.

"I've been dreaming about a world full of magic for as long as I can remember," said the empty space that was Marco. "But it's even better than I imagined."

"We like it," said Horace.

"I feel bad about squashing your windmill," Marco said then. "Especially now that I know it helps make cotton candy."

"Accidents happen," said Oona.

"Can you use your wand on it, Miss Fairy?" Marco asked.

"I think it has to be done the hard way. The cotton candy factory needs to be reliable, and"—Oona blushed—"reliable is not really my specialty, magic-wise. Except with underwear. And everyone knows underwear and cotton candy don't mix."

"Oh," said Marco, thinking. "What if I help you fix it?"

"I don't think we have time for that today."

"Let's just start it, then. We're waiting anyway, and it would make me feel a lot better about what I did."

Oona knew all about feeling guilty. She wouldn't wish that feeling on anyone. "Sure, we can start repairs."

Because Marco was so big, it was easy for him to move the heavy rocks that made up the walls of the windmill. As Marco stacked, Horace got the slugs to contribute slime to hold the boulders together. Oona worked on thatching the roof with bog reeds and twine. Before they knew it, a beautiful new windmill stood where the old broken one had been, its blades turning in the breeze. They had finished!

"Wow! We did it!" said Horace.

"Hey, Marco, can you lift up your underwear mask for a second so I can see your face?" asked Oona.

"Yes, Miss Fairy." Marco did as he was told, and two bright eyes appeared.

"I just wanted to say thank you. And"—she smiled—"you can call me Oona."

"Okay, Oona."

"And I'm Horace!" said Horace.

Marco laughed. "I know."

Then Oona yawned. "I don't know about you two, but I'm wiped out. I feel like I haven't slept in a month of Snorgledays! Let's take a break."

Marco sat down and carefully leaned against the new windmill, and Oona and Horace both leaned against Marco, which looked very odd since Marco was invisible. Before they could say *snickerdoodles*, they were all asleep.

The next thing Oona knew, someone was whispering in her ear.

"Rise and shine, friend," said Lucy. "Let's do this thing."

◦◦ ✦ ◦◦

CHAPTER ELEVEN

Within moments, they were all awake and moving, although Horace still looked like he wasn't quite sure how legs worked. But once Marco started asking him about slug stuff, Horace perked right up. Oona walked a few paces ahead with Lucy to work on the plan.

"How'd you fix it?" asked Oona.

"The slide? Oh, that was the easy part. A little dance party magic did the trick. Once I found a song the slide liked, it twisted itself right back together. The harder job was convincing my godmother that I needed more fairy dust."

"I've been wanting to talk to you about that," said Oona, twirling a curl nervously. "I don't think fairy dust is the best idea."

"What do you mean? We can't send him back home *remembering* everything," Lucy said, shaking her head. "Forgetting is essential to protecting this place."

"But we already tried fairy dust when I first met him, remember? He still told his friends about me. And built a trap!"

"That's why we're going to use a double dose," Lucy said.

"We can't," said Oona. "Not after what I heard today."

Lucy stopped then, and Oona stopped with her. The twisty slide was just around the next stand of trees. Lucy looked worried. "What did you hear?"

"He said he's been dreaming about magic for as long as he can remember! He's got magic inside him! If we give him a double dose of dust—"

"It will erase the magic from his heart," they finished together.

"Shoot. I don't want to do *that*," said Lucy.

"You don't want to do what?" asked Marco as he and Horace caught up to them.

"Um, we'll talk about it when we get there," said Lucy, hurrying on.

"Where are we going, anyway?" asked Marco, just as their destination appeared in front of them. There was the enchanted

waterfall, splashing droplets of glistening rainbows in the setting sun, with the top of the magical twisty slide behind it. What Oona hadn't anticipated was the long line of fairies of every shape and color standing by the ladder.

The Umbrella Fairy was first in line, in a fine orange suit with his net and cloud-collecting sack to prevent rain in places where humans had taken their nice dry umbrellas outside. The Crumb Fairy was next, trailing crumbs out of every pocket. She could hardly wait to add an extra hand-ful of crumbs to the bags of all the most delicious treats so they would last just a little bit longer.

The Shadow Fairy stood taller than the rest, dark and slinky, ready to transform every piece of furniture in a child's nighttime bedroom into a mysterious creature. She sometimes got her wires crossed between entertaining children and scaring them, but that was not unusual with shadow fairies. The Vacuum Fairy, the Puzzle Fairy, the Ice Cube Fairy—they were all in line. And they seemed to be getting impatient.

"I thought you said you fixed the twisty slide," said Oona.

"I did," Lucy replied.

"Then what's the holdup?" Oona wondered.

"Looks like it's a bossypants blockade," said Lucy, pointing.

At the base of the ladder, with a clipboard in one hand and a big red marker in the other, stood Molly.

$\backsim\!\!\diamond\!\!\backsim$

CHAPTER TWELVE

Lucy and Oona got in line behind the Dust Bunny Fairy, who was arguing with the Vacuum Fairy as usual. Since Horace was a Newbie, he was not supposed to go to the human world, so he stood off to the side. Just behind him, the grass was smushed down in a strange way. That was where Marco was waiting.

"We've got to get a move on. Snorgleday is almost over!" whispered Oona.

"It looks like she's just checking fairies

off her list; that shouldn't take too long. Let's not call attention to ourselves," Lucy whispered back.

"And no fairy dust, right?" said Oona.

Lucy shook her head. "I still haven't figured out how we'll keep Blackberry Bog from being exposed, though."

"I wish the Brainstorm Fairy was here," said Oona.

After five minutes, they had only moved a couple of feet. "What in fairydom is Molly doing up there?" Lucy asked. "Asking everyone to tell her a knock-knock joke? Hold our spot, Oona. I'll be right back." Lucy marched up to the front of the line.

Oona loved it when Lucy put Molly in her place. She didn't want to miss this.

"Horace," she said. "Hold our spot." She followed Lucy.

"Some of us have to get to work," Lucy was saying to Molly.

Molly turned to look at Lucy, raising

her magnifying glass. "It's called security. There's a giant threat."

"You know all these fairies! There's no giant threat here!"

Molly turned to Oona then and, surprisingly, put her arm around Oona's shoulder. "You understand, don't you, Underwear Fairy? After all, you're sort of in the security business yourself, right? Explain to your friend, please."

Wowee. Molly, the head of the fairy council, remembered who she was and what she did?! Oona was not at all prepared for this, but it made her feel good and nervous at the same time.

"Um, I'm sure we all want safety," Oona said. "But—"

"See, your friend is on the team," Molly interrupted, pointing her pen at Lucy. "And that's the kind of fairy we need around he—"

"AA-CHOOOOOOOO!"

A huge sneeze thundered from the back of the line. Everyone gasped and turned to look at what could have caused such a massive sound. Horace, looking surprised, wiped his nose and then let out a little "Ah, ah, choo. Choo. Bless you, I mean, me."

Molly eyed Horace suspiciously, then turned to Oona. "If your cousin has fairy fever, he should be home in bed. I expect you to—"

Horace couldn't claim *that* sneeze. It was so powerful it almost knocked the fairies in the middle of the line off their feet.

Molly jumped up on her puff of cloud. "That was no ordinary sneeze! It was a giant-sized sneeze. My fellow fairies, there is a giant in our midst! Protect yourselves!"

FUN FAIRY FACT: *Fairies are extremely healthy. The only illness they ever get is fairy fever. The symptoms of fairy fever are sneezing, purple spots on the soles of your feet, itchy earlobes, and an uncontrollable urge to shake your booty.*

The fairies all gasped again. They started looking every which way and waving their wands around. Oona and Lucy tried to get them to calm down, but the other fairies just ignored them. They were too busy freaking out.

The Umbrella Fairy magicked up an umbrella to float to safety. At the same time—*poof!*—the Vacuum Fairy made a vacuum and pressed the Blow button to push back any danger. Unfortunately, the blowing air caught the umbrella and flipped it inside out.

The Umbrella Fairy was furious and demanded that the Vacuum Fairy fix it immediately. So the Vacuum Fairy switched the magic from Blow to Suck, hoping to reverse the effect. But the suction was aimed directly at Marco.

It sucked the magical invisible underwear right off his head! Suddenly, his face was quite visible hovering over the cluster of fairies.

"There's the giant!" yelled Molly. "Get him!"

So the Vacuum Fairy got closer to Marco, sucking the underwear off his arms and front as well.

Oona had to do something, but she felt frozen. She whispered to her wand:

"Willaby wallaby woo,
The group can now see you.
To help you get away,
You need . . . you need . . ."

Oona was stuck. What did Marco need? A bale of hay? A leg X-ray? A nice bouquet? She shook her head. There was so much going on, she couldn't concentrate.

Meanwhile, Marco tried to escape, almost tripping over his own feet in his hurry, but an AUTO WEDGIE kept him upright before he flattened a whole bunch of fairies. Then the Shadow Fairy shot out shadowy vines from her wand that wrapped around him like a lasso. The other fairies grabbed the vines and started reeling him in like they were playing a claw game at the arcade and Marco was a stuffed animal.

Luckily, Horace ran up with a pair of golden scissors and clipped the vines, freeing Marco just in time.

"Keep going!" Horace shouted.

"Traitor!" Molly said, pointing to Horace. She broke free from Lucy, who had been trying to talk some sense into her, and raised her wand. Molly sometimes used tree frogs as messengers for fairy council business, and she summoned every one of them now. They surrounded Marco, a sea of little green heads looking up at him and ribbiting.

"THIS IS AN OFFICIAL SCOLDING," the frogs announced in a booming chorus, piling on top of one another.

Marco became invisible once more, but this time because he was covered by a mountain of frogs. A few steps away, a particularly loud frog backed Horace up against a tree trunk. They were trapped.

"Relax, friends!" Molly said, lowering her wand again. "I've captured the giant and kept you safe." Everyone except Oona, Lucy, Marco, and Horace clapped and cheered.

Molly bowed. "You're welcome. And now . . ." She paused here for effect. "We will secure Blackberry Bog once more."

‿〜 ✦ 〜‿

CHAPTER THIRTEEN

"Maybe we can keep him in an exhibit," Oona heard Molly say to the fairy council members. "So Newbie fairies can learn about the destructive nature of giants."

The other fairies, who had been panicking minutes ago, were now hovering around Marco,

plucking frogs off him so they could touch his hair and peer in his ears. Having never seen a giant before, they were fascinated. Every time Marco moved the tiniest bit, the fairies let out a half-scared, half-excited squeal.

A council member nodded. "And what about the traitor?"

"I'll have my scolding frogs fire him from his duties. We'll just have to find a new Slug Fairy," said Molly.

Oona's ears hurt at the very idea.

"We've got to do something. Anything," Lucy said. She opened her locket.

"I thought we agreed no fairy dust," said Oona.

"Not on Marco. But maybe it could make the other fairies forget? I mean, it doesn't seem to do anything when we touch it, but if we mix it with water and get them to drink it, it might just work."

Lucy magicked up a bottle and held it in the waterfall.

"No." As much as Oona wanted out of this, using magic against the other fairies felt like they were sinking in trouble quicksand. "I've got an idea."

Lucy raised her eyebrows. "What's that?"

Oona took a deep breath. "Truth bombs."

She stepped in front of Marco. "Excuse me, everyone. I have an important announcement. Excuse me! Hello?" With all their squealing, the other fairies didn't even notice Oona.

But Marco did. "Listen, everybody!"

Immediately, there was complete silence. Molly looked annoyed.

"Fairies, there's been a big mistake," Oona said. "This"—she swept her arm up toward Marco—"isn't a giant. This is a human child."

At that, all the fairies listening scrambled

backward. Even the frogs jumped away a bit. Everyone started asking questions.

"A human child! How did this happen?"

"What does he want?"

"I thought human children had tails." That comment came from the mostly magenta fairy, who had never been to the human world.

Then Molly's voice rang out above the others. "What are you playing at, Underwear Fairy? You told me yourself you saw a giant."

Oona swallowed. "I lied."

The other fairies' voices rose up again, louder and angrier, but Horace caught Oona's eye and gave her a little thumbs-up.

Molly raised her hands for quiet. "It can't be a human. It's much too small," Molly said to the group. "And how would a human get here, anyway? It's ridiculous."

"I shrunk him," said Oona. "And he came

up the slide on a magic carpet after I escaped from a trap he set this morning."

"Morning . . . trap . . . slide . . . shrunk?!?"
The amount of rules broken all at once had
Molly completely tongue-tied.

Her frogs, however, were not. Immediately,
more than a handful hopped over to unroll
their scolding scrolls at Oona's feet. "THIS
IS AN OFFICIAL SCOLDING," they boomed.

"I know, I know. I surrender
my wand for as long as you
think is best," Oona said,
laying the wand on
the ground.

Instead of it disappearing in a puff of smoke as it usually would, Molly picked it up herself and tucked it in her waistband. It seemed to give Molly great satisfaction.

Seeing her wand snuggled up against Molly made Oona's hands itch like she wanted to punch a pillow, but she knew she had no choice.

"And here I was thinking you were a safety-first kind of fairy," Molly said, shaking her head. "I am disappointed. I knew having an Underwear Fairy was a bad idea."

Oona's face burned. Lucy stepped up next to her. "Speaking of safety, let's stay focused. We have to get the boy back down the twisty slide right now, before Snorgleday is over and his parents realize he's missing. You of all fairies should know how important that is."

"And I suppose I'll have to clean up your fairy mess as usual," said Molly, putting on her bossiest voice. "First, give him an extra-large double dose of the Grands' fairy dust. Next, I will snap him back to size on his way down." She turned to the rest of the fairies. "Not to worry, friends. The fairy council has this whole thing under control."

Oona sighed. "We can't fairy-dust him."

Molly clenched her teeth. "Little fairy, you are going to make me lose my temper. Why in all of fairydom can't we dust him?"

"We have evidence he has magic in his soul."

Molly snorted. "That doesn't matter to me." She jumped down and pulled the locket right off Lucy's neck.

Molly was about to throw all the dust onto Marco when Horace yelled, "By the power of the Fairy Binder, I call for Rule Number 589G!!"

Molly stopped cold.

FUN FAIRY FACT: *The Fairy Binder contains all the fairy rules. It is 777 pages long, but almost nobody reads to the end. Some of the lesser-known fairy rules include Rule #121: Fairies should always hiccup into a bag and save it in case of future hiccup shortages, and Rule #314B: Fairy wands must never touch corduroy or cottage cheese. And of course, the last rule of the binder, Rule #702: Whenever the phrase "Guess what?" is said, the reply must be "Fairy butt."*

CHAPTER FOURTEEN

"No one has called for Rule Number 589G in three thousand years," Molly said, half to herself. Then she whipped around. "How do you know about Rule Number 589G?" she asked Horace.

Horace looked like he might throw up, but he kept his voice steady. "I've been reading the Fairy Binder."

"Why?"

"Because it's part of being a fairy, and I love everything about being a fairy."

Molly rolled her eyes. "Fine." She cleared

her throat. "Rule Number 589G states that any fairy may call a vote on any decision at any time as long as they have cotton candy in their bellies and their wings are in good working order."

Horace flapped his wings and patted his tummy.

Molly scowled. "Go ahead, Slug Fairy."

"Thank you, Miss Molly." Horace turned to the group. "Raise your hand if you think we should fairy-dust Marco, even though it could make him lose the magic in his heart."

"For the safety of the entire fairy world," added Molly.

With that last phrase, some of the fairies' hands started to creep up.

"Wait," said Oona. "Marco may have trapped and followed me, but that was before he really knew me. Or any of us. Once he started getting to know us, he only wanted to be helpful. And he wants more magic in his life! Isn't that right, Marco?"

"Totally," said Marco.

"If we send him back down with all his magic erased, he can't help anyone. But if we send him down as himself, he can help me find children who need protective undies! And he can help you, too! Puzzle Fairy, he could help you locate children who have lost the last piece of their puzzle. Shadow Fairy, he could tell you who the kids are that really love spooky, creepy stuff. He could help all of us!"

"Not me," said Molly. "My duties have zero to do with children. There is nothing for me in the human world."

"Well, maybe he could *discover* a way for you to help! Come on, everybody, we can trust him. It's a win-win!" Oona clasped her hands together. A lot of the other fairies were nodding.

"Let's count those hands again. Who votes for fairy-dusting?" Horace asked. Now none of the fairies raised their hands, not even Molly. A couple of frogs waved their hands in the air, but that was it.

"So it's settled," said Lucy. "Marco will return to the human world with magic alive in his heart. He'll be our representative there, and with his help, we'll find more children who need us." All the fairies cheered. Marco blushed.

The crowd of fairies and frogs cleared a path as Oona walked Marco to the slide.

"Are you ready?" she asked.

"I think so. Thanks for not letting them lock me up," he said.

"I'm here to help," said Oona.

"And I promise the secret of Blackberry Bog is safe with me."

"We'll be protecting each other from now on."

Marco looked down the slide. "I just wish I had something I could show my friends to prove to them I really had seen something incredible."

Just then, Horace came up next to Marco and placed two slugs on his shoulder. "How about these guys?"

Marco's mouth dropped open. "You mean I get to bring them home with me?"

Horace nodded. "They loved the human world. They want to live there. Plus, they're going to be our messengers, so when you find children needing help, the slugs will bring us their names. Okay?"

Marco's face clouded again. "What about children on the other side of the world who need you? My mom won't let me go past the traffic light at the corner without supervision."

"You can send the slugs on secret missions," Horace explained. "They are speedier than they seem."

FUN FAIRY FACT: *Magic slugs are a very close-knit team. They share everything except their toothbrushes. So when one slug needs to go super fast, that slug can borrow speed from another slug. That's why slugs often look so slow — it's not their turn to be speed demons.*

Oona smiled. "I'm guessing once you show a couple of friends your pet slugs that can slime a complete sentence, they'll forget all about the fairy sighting."

"Cool!" said Marco. He patted each slug's head. Then he asked, "Can I come back sometime?"

"Maybe some Snorgleday," said Oona. "We might have to call for Rule Number 589G again to make it happen. But I would like that."

"Me too," said Marco. "Okay, let's go, little slugs. Goodbye, fairy friends!"

As he headed down the slide, Lucy turned to Molly. "Do your thing."

Molly pretended she didn't hear her.

"Molly!"

"Oh, all right," Molly grumbled. "But I still think he would have made a great exhibit." She snapped her fingers three times. With each snap, Oona could see Marco expanding as he disappeared from view.

"There, see?" said Lucy to Molly. "You just helped your first child. How did it feel?"

At that, Molly straightened her shoulders. "Yes, I did, didn't I? It felt pretty good. That's me, Molly Malarkey, head of the fairy council and helper of children."

Once Marco was safely back in the human world, Horace linked arms with Oona and they turned toward home.

"Hey, Oo," he said. "Is it possible to feel proud of someone, even if they're bigger and older than you?"

Oona smiled and gave his palm a squeeze. "For sure. It's also possible to be proud of yourself, even if what you did got you punished."

Then she stopped. "Speaking of proud, I'm proud you're such a Fairy Binder expert!"

"Thanks!"

"I just have one question—where did you get those snazzy scissors? Shadow vines are notoriously hard to cut."

"I just magicked them."

"YOU MAGICKED THEM?!?"

Horace smiled and nodded.

"Horace! That's so exciting! You have magic now!" Oona danced around him in a circle. "How does yours work?"

"It's pretty easy. I think about what I want, and then I snoot."

"You what?"

"Snart?" asked Horace, unsure if that was a better word.

"Horace, what in fairydom are you talking about?" asked Oona.

"You know, when you sneeze and toot at the same time. You snoot."

"So you have to toot to make magic?"

"And sneeze. Together. Yes."

Oona tousled his hair. "Of course you do, Horace. You, Cousin, are a Bramblegoop through and through."

CHAPTER FIFTEEN

The next day, all the fairies worked together to fix the rest of the damage in Blackberry Bog. Oona, Horace, and Lucy were replacing broken stones in the wishing well when, suddenly, Lucy took out her locket and dropped it in.

"What did you do that for?" asked Oona, staring down at the ripple of water below.

"Some magic causes more trouble than it solves, and I think using fairy dust might fall in that category, at least for me."

Lucy shrugged. "Maybe you have to be a Grand to use it well." Lucy squinted down at where the locket disappeared and whispered something.

Oona wondered if it was a wish.

At that moment, Horace squealed. "It's Squeegee and Smoosh!"

"What?" Lucy and Oona said together.

"You know, the slugs that went to the human world with Marco." Sure enough, two slugs had slimed up and were sitting on the tops of Horace's shoes.

Horace picked up the slugs and held them close to his face. Although Oona and Lucy couldn't hear anything, Horace seemed to be listening to an exciting story. He kept laughing and shouting, "Wow!" and "Holy guacamole!"

"What are they saying?" Oona couldn't stand the suspense any longer.

"The slugs have already found three new children who need you, Oona!" said Horace.

"Plus, Marco introduced Squeegee and Smoosh to his whole class. The kids were so impressed, they started calling him Marco the Magnificent!"

"Wow, that wishing well works faster than I thought," said Lucy. Then, "Ugh, why do we always get bad news with good news?"

Molly was coming, and she looked mad. She started scolding them before she was even within earshot. They finally heard— "You have more to answer for." Molly stopped in front of them, caught her breath, and then started scolding again. "If there was no giant invasion, how do you explain the glitterberries? Did you let the human child take them?"

Lucy, Horace, and Oona all exchanged looks.

"What about the glitterberries?" asked Lucy.

"The entire glitterberry warehouse has

been cleaned out. Not one glitterberry left."
Molly folded her arms. "We need them
returned at once."

"Crudmuffin," said Oona. "That wasn't us.
Or Marco."

"Which means," said Lucy, brushing
back her braids, "we've got another problem to solve. We're here to help, Molly. But
don't you think you should give Oona her
privileges back, just until we find the thief?
We'll be more efficient that way."

Molly rolled her eyes but pulled out the
wand. "For efficiency only. No funny fairy
business," she said, handing it to Oona and
hustling away.

"You're so good at talking to her," Oona said
to Lucy. "Thank you." Oona gave her wand a
big kiss.

"Hey, I did it for all of us," said Lucy. "No
one knows better than me how your sideways magic and upside-down ideas can be

just what the dentist ordered. Not to mention your new secret weapon."

"My new secret weapon?" asked Oona.

"Truth bombs." Lucy grinned. "Now, let's get to work."

Turn the page for a sneak peek
at the next book in the series!

OONA BRAMBLEGOOP'S SIDEWAYS MAGIC

Fairies vs. Leprechauns

✧

CHAPTER ONE

From outside the glitterberry warehouse, everything seemed normal. Festive garlands of daisies and forget-me-nots hung from the eaves, gravel made of rainbow sprinkles crunched lightly under their feet, and the "Glitter Jitterbug" song bounced out of speakers near the front door, just like always.

But Oona and her friends knew something was very, very wrong.

"We need to get inside," said Oona as she and her cousin Horace crouched in some ferns.

Oona's best friend, Lucy, peeked at the warehouse from behind a tree, the tips of her long wings peeking out, too. "We don't have a key."

"Ooh, let me," said Horace, and he whistled a silent slug call. Horace was the Slug Fairy, and the slugs of Blackberry Bog were devoted to him. Instantly, several slugs appeared at Horace's side. He whispered to them where ears would be if slugs had ears. Then the slugs scooched over to the warehouse door. Flattening themselves into slug pancakes, they slid underneath.

"Boy, I do not remember them being so helpful back when I was Slug Fairy," said Oona. She was proud of her cousin, but she had been Slug Fairy before him, and the fact that he was better at the job than she'd ever been wasn't her favorite.

Horace shrugged. "It's easier if you think like a slug. The most important thing to them is—" He was interrupted by the creak of the warehouse doors swinging open.

"Looks clear," said Lucy. "Let's go."

Earlier that day, the glitterberry warehouse had been robbed, emptied of every last glitterberry, and Molly, head of the fairy council, had accused Oona, Lucy, and Horace of being involved, even though they were totally innocent. Oona understood why it might be hard for Molly to trust them, though, considering that they had recently broken about a dozen Fairy Binder rules by accidentally bringing a human boy with them into the fairy world and then making him invisible to try to cover it up.

So, to clear their names, and because they were naturally helpful fairies, they had offered to help solve the mystery and get the glitterberries back.

Oona looked forward to finding the berries. She loved a little glitterberry cake at the end of a long night of her work as the Underwear Fairy. But more than that, she was excited to impress Molly.

"Molly was right," said Lucy as they looked around the empty building. "Not a single glitterberry left. Not even a squished one."

Lucy didn't say Molly was right very often. Since Lucy was the Tooth Fairy, and therefore the most important fairy of all, Lucy and Molly didn't get along very well. They each thought the other was too big for her fairy pants.

"But whoever took them is long gone," Lucy continued.

"Time to investigate," said Oona.

FUN FAIRY FACT: *Glitterberries start out as regular black-berries. Blackberry Bog, the capital of the fairy world, has plenty of those. After the berries are picked, they are taken to the warehouse, dunked in Secret Syrup, and rolled in sweet sparkles collected from the moment sunlight hits the spray of the magic waterfall. Then the berries are spread out to crystallize on giant cookie sheets.*

Horace saluted. Then, looking very serious, he began sniffing the windowsills and listening to the refrigerators. He even licked an empty berry box.

Oona rolled her eyes. "Horace, what in fairydom are you doing?" As usual, Horace's uniqueness was getting on her nerves.

"I'm searching for clues," Horace said, his face very close to the berry-dunker machine.

"You're just trying to find food," Oona said. Horace loved to eat, and he loved eating glitterberries most of all.

"Not just food. *Investigation* food," said Horace.

Oona sighed and opened a closet door, clicking on the light. Horace squealed. "A clue!" He scampered past her and picked up something small and green.

Oona and Lucy gathered around him. "A four-leaf clover?" Lucy said. "What's that doing in the closet?"

By day, **KATE KORSH** has been a mild-mannered elementary school teacher, an insightful marriage and family therapist, and a cuddly mother of two, with no magic whatsoever. But by night, she has studied the magical world of creative writing. The Oona Bramblegoop's Sideways Magic series is the culmination of her studies. Kate lives in Los Angeles with her husband and the aforementioned cuddle recipients, who now always seem to magically have clean underwear in their drawers.

@korshkate

MARTA ALTÉS is the author and illustrator of many books for children, including the Dork Lord series by Mike Johnston and the picture books *My Grandpa* (an Ezra Jack Keats New Illustrator Honor book), *Little Monkey*, and *Five More Minutes*. Originally from Barcelona, she received her MA in children's book illustration at the Cambridge School of Art, and lives in London with her family. Marta hopes for Oona to visit them very soon, because she is notoriously clumsy.

Marta-Altes.com
@martaltes